One hundred and fifty years ago, on 7 September 1838, Grace Darling helped her father rescue passengers and crew from a stricken ship. Very soon after, her courage and heroism were being praised and celebrated all over Britain. And ever since her name has been associated with extreme bravery. But who was this extraordinary young woman and what was her life like in the remote lighthouse off the wild Northumberland coast?

In this moving and atmospheric story of her life, Helen Cresswell describes how Grace grew up on the Farne Islands and in the nearby coastal village of Bamburgh with its great castle; how she grew to love the sea-birds and learnt the legends of that ancient coast; and how at the age of ten she and her family moved to a new lighthouse on a lonely flat rock in which her room was eighty feet above the waves.

And in dramatic detail she recounts the events which made Grace a national heroine – the sinking of the *Forfarshire* in a violent storm and Grace's part in rescuing the survivors.

Throughout the intervening years, Grace Darling's story has stirred children's imaginations and this wonderfully evocative retelling is the perfect celebration of the 150th anniversary of her heroism.

The Royal National Lifeboat Institution will receive a small part of the proceeds from the sale of this book for its Grace Darling Appeal.

Helen Cresswell was born in Nottinghamshire and was educated there and at King's College, London. She now lives in an old farmhouse in Robin Hood country with her family. Of the more than forty books she has written some have been televised and four were runners-up for the Carnegie Medal.

HELEN CRESSWELL

THE STORY OF
GRACE DARLING

ILLUSTRATED BY
PAUL WRIGHT

PUFFIN BOOKS

PUFFIN BOOKS

Published by the Penguin Group
27 Wrights Lane, London W8 5TZ, England
Viking Penguin Inc., 40 West 23rd Street, New York, New York 10010, USA
Penguin Books Australia Ltd, Ringwood, Victoria, Australia
Penguin Books Canada Ltd, 2801 John Street, Markham, Ontario, Canada L3R 1B4
Penguin Books (NZ) Ltd, 182–190 Wairau Road, Auckland 10, New Zealand

Penguin Books Ltd, Registered Offices: Harmondsworth, Middlesex, England

First published 1988
Published simultaneously in hardback by Viking Kestrel
1 3 5 7 9 10 8 6 4 2

Filmset in Monophoto Palatino
Made and printed in Great Britain by
Butler & Tanner Ltd, Frome and London

Puffin edition printing at Cox & Wyman

Dedicated to the brave men of
the Royal National Lifeboat
Institution, past and present.

CONTENTS

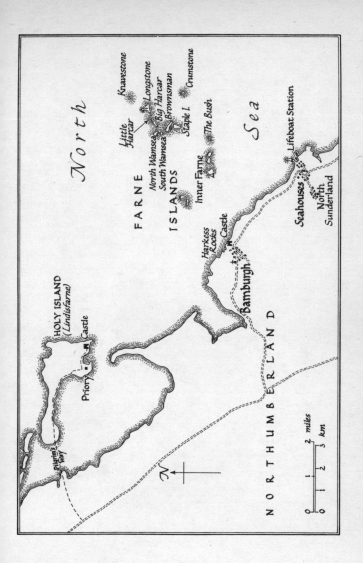

PROLOGUE

Go to the little village of Bamburgh in Northumberland, and you can still see the house where Grace Darling was born. There are lines of low stone cottages by a large triangular green, called the Grove, thickly planted with trees. The skyline towards the sea is dominated by the castle, massive and towering, its stones curiously tinged with pink, the walls haunted by screaming sea-birds. Beyond lie the pale sands and the deep, heaving waters of the North Sea. The rollers, smooth as glass, rise and fall and splinter.

If you stand on the high ridge facing seaward and look to your left, you can see the Holy Island, Lindisfarne, where Christianity first came to Northumbria. Then, if you move your gaze towards the right, you see the cruel black shapes of the Farne Islands, like broken-backed monsters rising from the water. You can see the Brownsman, where the first lighthouse in the Farne Islands was built, and where Grace Darling spent the first ten years of her life. Beyond is the Longstone, where the Darlings moved in 1826, and where you can see the tall red and white pillar of the present lighthouse, its light ceaselessly flashing. It warns of hidden

rocks, double tides, treacherous currents. The waters about it
are the grave of countless sailors, wrecked within sight of
land and safety. This is a cruel sea.

Then turn about and look inland. There lies Bamburgh
with its cottages and trees. It is another world, harmless and
everyday. Go down from the ridge and walk through the
village. Smells of cooking drift from open doors, washing
billows on clothes-lines, cats are sunning themselves on warm
stones. The only hint of omen is the presence of the rooks,
scores of them, wickedly black and uttering their harsh cries.

Walk up past the shady Grove and you come to a high,
red brick wall, oddly out of keeping with the stones of the
village. Follow its curve round to the right and you come to
the house where Grace Darling was born. It is at the very
end of the village, and was the home of her grandparents,
Job and Grace Horsley. Opposite is the church of St Aidan
and the graveyard with the sea beyond. The view from the

windows is almost exactly the same as it would have been a hundred and fifty years ago and more. Almost. Now, you can see a great stone memorial with its effigy of Grace Darling herself, lying stiff and blind in stone, a long oar by her side.

But when that baby was born in this thick-walled cottage all those years ago, who could have known what destiny had in store for her? Who could have known that she was to risk her life in mountainous seas, to do a man's most dangerous work and astound a nation?

In every life there are turning points, crossroads. If at a certain time and in a certain place your mother had not met your father, you yourself would not exist. At the moment when Grace Darling was born those whom she was destined to save from death were going about their everyday business, quite unaware that their lives had been brushed by the distant birth of an unknown child. The great ship on which they were to set sail all those years later, the *Forfarshire*, had not yet been built. But on 7 September 1838 that ship and that unknown baby were together to make history, and there would be another birth – that of a heroine.

CHAPTER
1

BEGINNINGS

William Darling, ten years-old, had his father's telescope to his eye. He sat huddled on a rock, the air was clammy on his face and hands.

They'll come today, I reckon, he told himself. The sea was quiet – for November. The grey waves licked the rocks below him and sent up a mere spit of spray. It was misty – he could not even make out the bulky shape of the castle on the mainland, but mist, he knew, did not matter.

'They'll come the first day there's a quiet sea,' his father had said. By 'they' he meant Mr Lock and Mr Blackett, who came out often to the Brownsman with news and supplies. This time they would be coming to fetch Mrs Darling ashore. She was going back to the mainland to her parents' house in Bamburgh.

'Now there are six of you – soon there will be seven!' Mr Darling had announced only the week before.

Robert and Betsy were too young to know what he meant, but the other children immediately set up a hubbub.

'*That*'s nothing!' said William loftily. As eldest, he could remember there being only three of them – then four, then five, then six. And each time his mother had gone to the mainland to fetch the new baby.

'I'll be mother while you're gone,' said Thomasin, who as second eldest spent most of her time playing mother to the little ones, in any case. Someone had to make sure they didn't tumble into the sea while their mother was busy in the kitchen.

'That's it, my dear,' said her mother. 'And you must all be a help to your father.'

'Is it to be a girl or a boy, mother?' asked Mary Ann.

'A boy,' said William promptly. 'A boy, who can take an oar and help keep the lamp.'

'A girl, a girl!' chanted Thomasin and Mary Ann.

'Now just bide and see,' Mr Darling told them. 'There's three of each now — three boys, three girls. And whichever this new one is, it'll be welcome.'

This was true. The Darling family were the only inhabitants of the Brownsman island, which was so tiny that it was really no more than a rock. All they had for company besides one another were the birds, a few sheep and goats, rabbits and the sea itself. The sea was as much part of them as the air they breathed. At high tide it even came into the kitchen.

William had been on his rock now for nearly an hour, from time to time putting the glass to his eye. He meant to be lighthouse keeper himself one day, and that life would mean many patient hours of watching, day and night — and especially night. Already his father trusted him to take watches in the lantern room. Already he had rowed out and helped bring back sailors whose craft had foundered on the Harcars or Crumstone or the Knavestone rock.

Again he put the glass to his eye. He trained it steadily landward scanning the grey waves, seeing gulls, cormorants and guillemots so close that he felt he could put out his hand

and touch their feathers. And then —

'Ahoy!' he yelled. 'Ship ahoy!'

He made out the dim shape of the coble away out there in the mist.

'Where! Let's see!' Thomasin was there by his elbow and trying to pull the telescope from his grasp. He pushed her off.

'No! Wait!'

He wanted to see himself the magical moment when the name of the coble, *Seaventurer*, would make itself under his very eyes. He wanted to see the blurred shapes at the oars turn into real people, familiar faces. There! Now he could see the foxy whiskers of Mr Blackett, the red hair frizzing under his cap. And there was Mr Lock with his watery blue eyes and his lips moving as if he were singing.

'I see them but they don't see me!'

That was the power and the magic of the glass.

'Here — you can look now!' He thrust it into his sister's hand and scrambled to his feet stiffly, the cold in his bones.

'They're here!' he shouted. 'Mother, father, they're here!'

Soon the whole family had gathered, as they always did to greet visitors. On the Brownsman visitors were few and they seemed to come from another world.

As the coble drew close William caught the rope thrown to him and pulled the boat in. He threaded it through the great iron ring by the rocky steps and knotted it firmly.

Then the sailors set about unloading the provisions they had brought. First, and most important, were the barrels of drinking water. The Darlings collected rainwater in underground tanks, but carefully rationed the precious water from the mainland. None of the children were allowed to touch it.

'Man can live without bread, if need be,' their father would say, 'but not without water. Remember that.'

Sometimes the Brownsman was cut off from the mainland for weeks on end by gales and towering seas. Their provisions dwindled, their sacks of flour and oats, but it was always the water that Mrs Darling most anxiously eked out, drop by drop.

Now the coble was reloaded, this time with gifts from the Darlings to their family and friends on shore. There were boxes of salted fish, codlings and haddock. There was a quilt stuffed with feathers from the eider-duck for Grandpa Horsley, and a thick woollen waistcoat. Then Mrs Darling, bundled in shawls, was herself helped down into the boat.

'Make sure it's a girl, mother!' called Thomasin.

'Oh *you*, throng Tommy!' retorted William. 'We can do without any more throng Tommys, thank you! You fetch a boy back, mother!'

He untied the rope and tossed it to Mr Blackett, who caught it deftly. And just then the air lightened and the sun broke through, the mists shone yellow.

'Take care, mother!' called Mr Darling, as the two men took their oars.

And the children chanted as their mother was drawn away, 'A girl, a girl! A boy, a boy!' and their voices drifted to her over the waves long after she could make out her children's faces.

And so Grace Darling was born on shore. When she was older she would say that she wished she had been born on the Brownsman.

'Then I would have hatched out there on the rocks like a gull,' she said, 'or a kittiwake!'

'Such nonsense, Grace!' her mother told her. 'Hatched indeed! Whatever would good Dr Fender say to that? He fetched all your brothers and sisters into the world!'

Not *all* my brothers and sisters, Grace would think. Not all the puffins and rabbits and gulls, and not the kittiwakes either!

Grace Darling was born on 24 November 1815. She was baptized by the Reverend Andrew Boult in St Aidan's Church on 17 December, and then Mr Darling took his wife and baby daughter back to the Brownsman for Christmas.

Grace might have been born on land but she was, right from the beginning, a water child. The sea was her element, it bounded her world. She knew it in all moods and all seasons and the sound of it filled her ears day and night. In winter the setting sun would send over it paths of red fire. On moonlit nights the waves would gleam like puckered pewter. Sun and shadow chased over it in huge rolling bands. Grace knew the shallow rock-pools and she knew too that the sea was deep, fathoms deep, and that men drowned in its depths.

Grace crawled and took her first tottering steps among crowds of sea-birds and so thought of them always as part of the family. Brownsman is divided only by a narrow strait from Staple Island, whose jagged rocks rise steeply from the sea. They are of dark whinstone and called the Pinnacles, and are so whitened by bird droppings that they seem to be covered in snow all year round. Birds flock there by the thousand, clinging impossibly to toe-holds on the sheer rock face. Grace would look over there and see the puffins, razor-bills and guillemots, standing upright and flapping their wings as if in greeting. Grace would wave back and call out to them, and their low grunts would be blown back to her in answer.

Sometimes there were storms and the Pinnacles would be blotted out by walls of water and blown spray. The whole world would seem to turn to water. Grace would lie at night wide-eyed, listening to the roar of wind and sea, and could hardly believe she would ever see her friends again. But the

storm would blow itself out and Grace would run outside and there they all would be, tiptoe on their rock, flapping their dark wings as if to say, 'We're the kings of the castle!'

The puffins on Brownsman itself would waddle in lines playing follow-my-leader, and Grace would follow, though never too far. Her elder sisters, Thomasin and Betsy, kept a sharp eye on her. When she was very little they tethered her like a goat. She tugged and tugged at the twine tied to her apron strings and screamed till her face was wet and scarlet. But in the end she gave up and started to poke about in the little rock-pools, and scratched the moss from the stones with a stick. She behaved, in fact, exactly like a bird, and her own eyes grew nearly as sharp as theirs.

She learnt to know all the birds and animals on the Browns-man as if they really were her brothers and sisters. She learnt to tell the lesser black-backed gulls and the herring-gulls apart. They were greedy, and often swooped down on other birds' eggs and snapped them up. They took their rest on the water, bobbing out there in the long hours of darkness. She liked the smaller gulls, especially the kittiwakes, so called because their cry seemed to say, 'Kitty *wake*, Kitty *wake!*' They built their nests on the sheer cliffs, nests of trampled seaweed on the tiny ledges. Below them the tide roared ceaselessly into the crevasses, white and boiling. All day, every day, the air was filled with the cries of sea-birds.

Grace spent the first ten years of her life on the Brownsman. She took for granted the queer Robinson Crusoe-like way of life. All the Darlings did. They had a world of their own on that tiny, windswept island, and like Robinson Crusoe had to keep themselves as best they could.

The twins, George Alexander and William Brooks, arrived four years after Grace, and so there were eleven mouths to feed at the beginning. Sometimes there were shipwrecked sailors rescued by Mr Darling, and they would have to be looked after on the island until they recovered or until the sea calmed.

There was a little coarse grass on the island, enough to graze a few sheep, and goats for their milk. There were also, oddly, thousands of rabbits — how did they get there, Grace would wonder? Did they swim over from Bamburgh, or even fly on the backs of gulls? She loved them, and would creep away and cover her ears when her father and brothers went out to shoot them. She kept out of the kitchen while her mother and Betsy or Thomasin skinned and drew them ready for the pot. On Pot Days (every Sunday, and sometimes other special occasions) the family would always sit down to a meat dinner with broth and dumplings and plenty of vegetables.

Mr Darling and his older sons worked hard at the garden. They built a stone wall round the patch of thin soil to protect it from the wind and waves. They grew potatoes, carrots and turnips, cabbages and rhubarb. Even so, their crops were often destroyed by spring tides, and they would have to begin sowing all over again. Sometimes the catastrophes were recorded in Mr Darling's journal:

'Two tremendous gales viz. April 1st, west with snow showers; and on the 26th and 27th E. by N. severe with showers of sleet. The garden small seeds being all above ground were totally blown off or destroyed.'

Then, a few years later, 'A severe gale W. by N. from 10 a.m. till 4 p.m. destroyed nearly three-quarters of the Brownsman garden.'

The very next year 'A severe gale and high tide broke down part of the lower wall and overflowed the soil.'

There was a plague of earwigs:

'I caught frequently one quart in the evening by placing cabbage leaves on the ground and laying a little barley meal in the middle and emptying them among hot water.'

There were plenty of wild birds for food, and in the winter, when the island was often cut off for weeks on end, Mr Darling and his sons would go out with their guns. They shot wild duck, teal and widgeon. In the summer months Grace and her sisters would search for gulls' eggs, some for the family and the rest to be sent ashore. These were about four times bigger than hens' eggs, but eaten warm were rather strong in taste – they had a 'fang', as people said. They would usually be eaten cold for breakfast.

The Darlings' real larder was the sea, always on their doorstep. There was codling, herring and haddock to be eaten fresh or salted down for the winter. From an early age all the Darling children learnt to take an oar and row with their father among the scattered Farnes with net and line.

Mrs Darling taught all her daughters to cook and to make bread and scones with wheaten flour, oats and barley and pease flour. They made Northumbrian girdle-cakes or 'singing hinnies' – so called because of the sound they made as they sizzled on the hot girdle. Then there were crowdies and hasty pudding, made with oatmeal. Home-made jams and butter came from the mainland in exchange for fish and eggs or eiderdown. Money rarely changed hands, as the Darlings lived by bartering.

Mrs Darling had a spinning wheel and the girls learnt to spin and weave the stuff for the family's clothing. Thomasin was a good needlewoman, and later set up in Bamburgh as a dressmaker. When Grace was five the twelve-year-old Thomasin taught her little sister to sew, and the pair of them spent hours together stitching and chattering and singing the old border ballads.

Mr Darling, of course, had his duties as lighthouse keeper. The lighthouse itself was forty-three feet high, with an oil lamp and a revolving reflector light that gave a bright flash every half-minute. The chimney and reflectors were of silvered copper mounted on an iron frame and driven by clockwork. It was Mr Darling's first duty to keep his light in perfect order day and night, three hundred and sixty-five days a year. Every day the reflectors were polished and the wicks trimmed. Grace often helped her father in these tasks, and as they worked he told her stories of old wrecks, or of his exploits as a smuggler when a young man.

The lantern room was like the bridge of a ship. Down below the thick walls kept out the roar of the wind and waves, but up in the lantern with its hollow roof the light and noise were tremendous. On every side were flying spray and birds, and in high winds often the birds were blown off course to crash into the windows of the lantern itself. On clear days Grace could see the busy traffic of boats and the surrounding islands, each with its white ruff of spray.

Mr Darling kept a record of all ships sighted. This was one of the lighthouse regulations:

'A book containing a note of the vessels passing each lighthouse shall be kept; and an annual schedule, showing the number of vessels in each month, shall be sent.'

Record was kept of vessels that foundered and lives saved. Ships of every kind shuttled back and forth daily past the Farne Islands in the days before the railways. There were brigs, barques, sloops and schooners, packets, smacks and keels. The packets carried mail and passengers; the keels were flat-bottomed coal barges from Newcastle. The local fishing-boats were known as cobles.

Mr Darling was paid thirty shillings a week. In addition to this he received salvage, a payment for anything he saved from the sea. The Darling boys would row in and out the islands after a spell of rough weather, looking for any odd oars or nets or boxes of cargo that had been swept overboard. These they took into the nearby harbour of Seahouses. If the owners claimed them, they would pay a small reward.

There was always work to be done by every member of the family, they were always busy − or 'throng'. Grace had little time for play, and in spare moments ran over the island with her pet dog, Happy. She poked in the little pools left by the tide for shells and later began a collection of birds' eggs. She began to keep her own journal, in which she noted the birds she saw, their species and habits. She noted, for instance, that one year all the guillemots returned a month earlier than usual. She noted that every night the terns would all rise between eleven and midnight with a tremendous noise, exactly as they did between eleven and noon. Why, she wondered? What mysterious clock did these wild birds obey? They made patterns through the hours as well as in the air. They swooped and dived and then, all of a sudden, became absolutely quiet. Then they would rise all together high into the air, and sweep in procession out to sea, the only sound the beat of their long wings.

Grace noted that oyster-catchers lined their nests with winkle shells and other tiny shells from the beach, arranging them in a curious mosaic. She crept up close to watch the puffins, or sea parrots. They were clumsy and bumbling on land, and often rolled over and over till they reached the cliff edge and tumbled into the sea. William told her that they waddled so clumsily because they had pins and needles, but she hardly knew whether to believe him.

When she was five Grace had a pet eider-duck who fed from her hand and followed her everywhere. Her father told her that eider-ducklings went straight from the shell into the sea. Their mothers led them into the water and kept them there for three days, to make them hardy and able to fend for themselves. Later, Grace watched this for herself. At the moment those tiny birds went follow-my-leader after their mother into that wild sea, Grace caught her breath and shut her eyes. Next minute she would open them, and there the brood would be, bobbing and riding the waves.

But I couldn't do that, she would think, and shiver. I'd be frightened.

And so Grace Darling grew up knowing the sea but never, deep in her bones, trusting it.

BAMBURGH

During the years on the Brownsman there were some occasions when the Darlings would visit the mainland, and the most exciting of these was the annual St Aidan's Feast in Bamburgh. For the family it was a last outing before winter closed in and their lives were bounded by grey seas and storms.

The feast was in late August. The leaves were turning, they glowed yellow and rust and their colours amazed the Darling children whose world was of muted greys and browns and blues. Everyone kept open house for three days and people flocked from miles around. The Grove was lined with stalls selling gingerbread, nuts, oranges and sweetmeats. There were booths where boots and shoes were sold, and the whole family would be fitted up for the year ahead. There was hardware, cutlery and crockery. Shepherds came down from their lonely folds in the Cheviots to buy tar in barrels. All kinds of sports were played, like ninepins and quoits.

Grace herself sometimes visited Bamburgh alone to stay with Job Horsley in the house where she had been born. Job's cottage stood directly behind a large walled garden. This belonged to the Crewe Trustees of Bamburgh Castle, where Job was head gardener. After the ceaseless buffeting of wind and waves on the island, that sheltered garden with its high, rosy walls was like another world, hushed and windless. Grace spent hours there as a small child, following her grandfather.

He moved slowly about his tasks, as much at home there as Grace was in the lighthouse. He had his kingdom there, just as William Darling had his kingdom on the Brownsman. It seemed to Grace afterwards that it had always been summer there. Fruit trees were trained against the walls, bearing luscious fruit that could never have survived the icy blasts on the island. There were plump pears, golden nectarines, apricots and peaches. Grace picked them herself and sank her teeth in them so that the juices ran down her chin.

Job taught her how to dibble the earth and set seeds. She learnt to catch slugs and earwigs, and to wind string between twigs to keep off the birds.

The world within those walls was safe and calm, but the world outside them seemed wide and dangerous.

The village of Bamburgh itself seemed safe enough, to begin with. When Grace looked out of her window she could see a range of hump-backed hills to her left, a green dragon. Opposite was St Aidan's Church and the graveyard, and beyond that the wide shine of the North Sea. Each morning Grace ran straight to the window for a reassuring glimpse of that sea, which was her home.

On Sundays, wearing her best clothes, Grace would go to church with her grandfather. She walked between the leaning gravestones, barnacled like rocks and strangely blooming with moss. As she sat stiffly in her pew she would look up at the broad, curved rafters and imagine herself in a great ship.

Sometimes Grace would watch from behind the shutters

of the cottage as a funeral procession wound through the graveyard. The group of black-clad mourners stood by the open grave while the gulls and rooks clamoured and rode the wind.

'Who is it?' Grace would ask, and the answer, as often as not, was a sailor or fisherman, drowned at sea.

The low stone cottages of Bamburgh stood around a large, triangular green, thickly planted with trees and known as the Grove. On the Brownsman there was not a single tree. It was all light and space, bright salty air.

If you ventured into the Grove the sky disappeared, the air was dim and green. The sun came sifting through the moving leaves in flakes. If she stood absolutely still, holding her own breath, Grace would think that she could actually hear the trees breathing, whispering even. She would turn and run, back into the light, back to the safety of the cottage. But each time she knew she would be drawn back to that mysteriously breathing place. She dared herself, played cat and mouse with herself, risked the rising fear, the hard pounding of her heart.

And then she began to hear the stories. At first she heard only snatches, and if the grown-ups saw her they would lower their voices or break off altogether. She caught odd words — demons, wreckers, the Worm. And the silences between these words were more frightening than the words themselves. They left a space for Grace to fill with her own imaginings.

She learnt, whisper by whisper, that the stretch of Northumbrian coast where Bamburgh lies is a strange and haunted place. She sensed it, in the red, flaring sunsets, in the deserted landscape that seemed to watch and wait.

Grace learnt first that St Aidan had brought Christianity to Northumbria, after Oswald had defeated the Pagans. He was given Lindisfarne, a tiny island just north of Bamburgh, and there established his church. Lindisfarne is separated from the mainland by a narrow strip of land known as the Pilgrim's Way. When the tide is high, the sea rushes in to cover it, and woe betide the traveller who sets off across it without consulting the tide timetables. Local people told stories of unearthly sightings of lines of hooded monks, chanting and walking steadily over the waters from Lindisfarne at sunset.

'They walk over that Pilgrim's Way even when the tide be at full flood,' they said. 'And we see them clear as we see you now, though we don't see their faces for the pulled-up cowls. And we hear them chant, and enough to freeze the blood in your veins. But though they walk on water they leave no print – there's no reflections! Think of it!'

Grace did think of it, though she tried hard not to. They took her one day in the cart to Lindisfarne. The Pilgrim's Way lay bare and innocent in the silvery sea light, but still in her mind's eye she could see those monks in deliberate procession.

'If you hear the tolling of a bell, cover your ears and cover them tight!' her grandfather told her. 'It's an ill omen when a bell tolls out from Lindisfarne. It means the devil's abroad.'

The devil's abroad! The words rang like a knell in Grace's ears. On nights when the gales blew into Bamburgh from the north-east, she would cover her ears with her hands and burrow deep beneath her eider quilt.

There were stories told of St Cuthbert, who came after St Aidan to Holy Island. Some she liked – those of his love for the wild creatures of the Farne Islands, the sea-birds and the seals. On the other hand, they said he had hated all women. He would not even allow his monks to keep cows on Lindisfarne.

'For where there is a cow, there must be a woman,' he said.

'And where there is a woman, there must be mischief.'

He even built a special chapel for women at the far end of Lindisfarne, so that they should not enter his church.

Grace liked the rest of this story, though. After Cuthbert died and was made a saint, his monks received a heavenly message from him, telling them where they should lay his remains and build a church. The name of the appointed place was Dunholm.

So the monks took up the coffin and set off over the Pilgrim's Way to look for this place. They wandered about the mainland, searching in vain. Then, discouraged, they laid down the coffin and rested awhile. Just then, they heard a woman who was searching for her cow call to another woman, asking if she had seen it.

'Aye, that I have!' she replied. 'It's yonder, in Dunholm!'

And she pointed out the place. So when St Cuthbert finally came to rest the monks were guided to the place by a woman. They first built a little church of wands and branches above the coffin. This was then replaced by a stone chapel, and then by a great white church. Finally, the magnificent, soaring Durham Cathedral was built in honour of the saint.

Grace was shown pictures of the church, and as she stared at it would think, 'And all because of a woman and her lost cow!'

The Farnes were the abode of saints but were the home too of other, darker spirits. For centuries they were associated with witchcraft and black magic. Local people would wisely say that this was to be expected.

'Wherever goodness is, there will the devil try his hardest,' they said. The demons had visited the Farnes to do battle with the monks and try to drive them out.

St Bartholomew, who came to Holy Island after St Cuthbert, himself wrote about the haunting of that coast:

From the east to the west it is begirt with rugged rocks and the boundless ocean, it labours under a constant struggle and invincible conflict with the waves. Here the demons are supposed to reside. The brethren ... have seen them in a sudden, clad in cowls and riding upon goats, black in complexion, short in stature, their countenance most hideous, their heads long, the appearance of the whole troop most terrible. Like soldiers they brandished their hand-lances which they darted after the fashion of war. At first the sign of the cross was sufficient to repel their attacks, but the only protection in the end was a circumvallation of straws signed with the cross, and fixed in the sand around which the devils gallowed for a while, and then retired.

Much later Grace read St Bartholomew's words herself, in a book borrowed from the library at the castle. But she first heard the stories by the fireside on long winter evenings, and from the games of the children.

One windy October day, towards sunset, a group of Bamburgh children called to Grace to come and play. They had been scrumping apples and pears all afternoon and were filled with the excitement of being chased, reluctant to go home in the lengthening shadows.

'Come on, come on, Grace Darling!' they called.

At first she shook her head. She was used only to the company of her own family and that of the wild birds on the Brownsman. The children of Bamburgh were rough and tough, quick to punch and kick and full of devilment. The sharp smell of autumn was in the air and they were drunk with it.

'Grace, Grace, daresn't show her face!'

'Darling, Darling, mammy's little Darling!'

'Come wi' us, and we'll show you the *devil*!'

Grace stood by the wall of the churchyard and hesitated. She felt a thrill of fear, the fear she felt when she crept alone into the Grove among the breathing trees. And just as she went back into the the Grove time after time to meet that fear, so now she knew she must go to meet this new terror. She saw that the village already lay in shadow. Only the topmost battlements of the castle were rosy in the last light. Soon the world would be swallowed in darkness.

Grace took a step forward.

'Daresn't! Daresn't!' taunted the largest boy.

'I dare, I dare!' cried Grace, and went to join them.

The pack of children began to run, tugging Grace along with them. Down the street and then to the left, down the Wynding to the sea. As they went the light faded, minute by minute. Soon the smell was not that of rotting leaves but that of the sea, salt and keen.

They left the Wynding and raced over the dunes with their clumps of coarse grass, and as they did so were met by the full roar of the North Sea breakers. The spray gleamed whitely in the gloom.

'Now for the devil, now for the devil!'

The children scampered hither and thither, flitting shapes on the pale sand.

'Grace Darling to be the saint! A goody-goody for saint!'

They formed a ring and pushed her into the middle.

'Stop there! Stand there and pray!' they shouted.

And then they turned and ran off, though still in a ring, a widening ring. Grace stood stock-still and dazed. She strained into the darkness and could see only skinny, jumping shadows with blurs for faces.

'Now beware, beware, beware ...' The whispers ran about her, mingled with the crash of breakers.

'We are the demons, and here we come a-gallowing!'

Grace stood rooted, her heart hammering. She was sur-rounded.

'We are the demons, and here we come a-gallowing!'

The shapes were advancing now, threatening, hands clawing at the air.

'Say your prayers and say them well, or else we'll fetch you down to hell!'

The voices hissed and the waves hissed and Grace would have fled, but she dared not break through that menacing ring. It seemed to her now that there were more shapes than there had been children. It seemed possible that the real demons had been called up, and were now assembling out of the darkness to join that dancing circle.

They were nearer now, step-stepping on the soft sand. Grace stood her ground.

And then, beyond the advancing shapes, Grace saw another, taller shape, further off but still taller and with an arm upraised. She screamed then, and pointed.

'Look! Look!'

For a split second the shadows froze into rocks or stones. And then the wide beach was filled with screaming and the ring broke and scattered.

'The devil! The devil! Help! Help!'

The terrified children streamed away, Grace with them, over the slithering dunes and up the Wynding, the devil at their heels. On they sped and did not stop till they reached the village and safety. Lights bloomed from the windows of the houses, dogs barked, pale smoke wreathed the chimneys.

'Off now – and don't tell!'

'Come on – fast!'

'Don't tell! Don't tell!'

The children sped away and Grace with them, up past the

Grove and beyond the churchyard with its littered stones, to burst breathless into her grandfather's kitchen.

Job sat by the fire, puffing at his pipe and whittling a stick. He lifted his head.

'Well now, our Grace,' he said, 'that's a wild look you've got. You'd think the devil was after you!'

Grace said nothing. She did not tell. Nor did any of those other Bamburgh children who were down on the shore that night. They had all seen that mysterious shape emerge from the darkness. It might have been just a man from the village, someone they knew, even. But secretly each and every one of them believed that as they played at demons gallowing, a real devil had come among them. And none of them ever told.

THE CASTLE

Bamburgh Castle stands on a high ridge on the very edge of the sea with pale sands sweeping beneath it. Birds nest and perch on the sheer walls like patches of snow in all seasons. The stone is a light rusty brown with bright-green waterfalls of lichen and moss. The little village lies quite literally in its shadow, and it is easy enough on dark days to believe the story of the Laidley Worm of Spindlestone. People claimed that the castle was still haunted by the loathsome beast.

Centuries ago, a king of Northumbria lived in Bamburgh Castle. He had two children – a beautiful daughter, Margaret, and a son, Childe Wynde. The old king had lost his first wife, but married again, a black-haired woman with cold eyes. No one in the castle liked this new wife, but Margaret was a favourite with everyone. The queen grew jealous. She waited until Childe Wynde had gone abroad to fight in a foreign war, and stole one night alone into the moonlit courtyard. There she whispered strange incantations and drew magical symbols on the stone.

Margaret lay sleeping in her chamber. She woke suddenly

to find the moon shining on her face and a foul taste in her mouth. She tried to rise, but her body was numb and heavy. Then a glint of silver caught her eye and she looked down to see a huge, taloned claw. Margaret screamed, but the sound she made was a thundering roar. She was no longer a young girl, but a foul worm.

The new-made dragon went slithering down the stone steps and out of the castle, and at dawn devoured a flock of sheep while the terrified people of Bamburgh watched from a distance. Then the worm made its way to a pillar of rock known as Spindlestone Heugh. There it wound its length into coils and basked in the sun.

As soon as news came that Margaret had disappeared, the people guessed that the jealous queen had spelled her into the worm. They consulted a sorcerer, who told them that Margaret could be released from the spell only by her brother, Childe Wynde.

He was sent for, and he came with his men sailing back to Bamburgh in a ship with a keel of rowan-wood to fend off evil spirits. As the turrets of the castle came into view the queen, watching from the high tower, made another spell. The dragon uncoiled itself from the Spindlestone and writhed over the fields towards the beach. It plunged into the sea and with lashing tail made for Childe Wynde's ship. It rammed the prow again and again, sending the terrified sailors flying. Childe Wynde saw that it was impossible to get past the dragon, so he pretended to give up and sail away.

But he sailed only a little way further down the coast, and landed in a small cove at Budle Bay. No sooner had he set foot on shore than there was a squalling of gulls, and then a thick poisonous mist rolled swiftly from the land, swallowing up Childe Wynde and his men.

They groped in the mist, arms outstretched as in blindman's buff. Then Childe Wynde saw, close up, a hideous eye, large and yellow as a lemon and set in wrinkled skin. He drew his sword but as he did so, heard his sister Margaret's voice telling him what he must do. And so he kissed that loathsome mouth, and as he did so the dragon slithered to his feet and lay there, an empty skin. In its place stood Margaret, fair and shining as before.

Childe Wynde set off for Bamburgh Castle and there found the queen cowering in her chamber. She had lost her magic powers at the moment when the rowan-wood prow had touched the shore. And Childe Wynde, with a wand of that same rowan-tree, turned her then into a speckled toad. It went hopping out of the castle and the queen was never seen again.

According to local legend, however, the spell could be lifted from the speckled toad, which still squats in a cavern beneath the castle. Once every seven years on Christmas Eve the portal of the cave opens, in case there is a brave man willing to kiss the toad and release the queen from her thraldom. And when the mists rolled in from the grey North Sea, silently enfolding the town, it was said that the phantom of the Laidley Worm slithered through the town to coil itself again round the Spindlestone. Whether it was true or not no one knew, for no one dared go and look.

Bamburgh Castle played a great part in the life of the town and in the lives of the Darlings themselves. It had been left by Lord Crewe in his will to be used for charity, especially in the field of education. It was run by the Crewe Trustees, who were chosen from among clergymen of Durham Cathedral, and their agent, who at that time was Mr Smeddle. They provided a 'Free Shop', where food and groceries were sold cheaply to the poor, and people came from distant farms and villages with their donkeys, to fill their basket paniers. There was also a little hospital, or infirmary, for local people and for the care of sailors who had been shipwrecked. Men who had lost all their belongings at sea would be newly fitted up with clothes before going on their way. The Crewe Trustees offered rewards for saving life at sea. They maintained the Bamburgh lifeboat and subscribed to the Newcastle Lifeboat Institute. They were actually responsible for the first attempt at a lifeboat station in England. They sent a local coble down to London to a Mr Lukin, a coachbuilder, and he converted it into an 'insubmergible boat'.

At the foot of the castle tower was a huge gun that was fired at regular intervals in fog, to warn mariners that they were approaching the dangerous rocks of the Farne Islands. There was also a bell in one of the turrets, rung in fog to guide local fishermen. In stormy weather two men on horseback went out to patrol the coast from dawn to dusk. If a ship in distress was sighted, one man would ride back to the castle to raise the alarm while the other stayed to mark the ship. A large flag was then raised on the castle tower so that the wrecked seamen would know that they had been sighted and help was on its way.

So Bamburgh Castle and Mr Darling were each playing an important part in the saving of life at sea.

But to Grace as a child Bamburgh Castle meant books. There were two schools in the castle. One was for boys, and educated them to become doctors, lawyers, navigators and schoolmasters. The other was a Charity School held in the great hall, and was for thirty poor girls. They were boarders, and wore a uniform of blue with a white collar. The only lessons they had were in simple arithmetic and writing. The rest of the time they learnt to knit, sew and spin, so that when they were sixteen they could go into service as maids.

Grace herself did not go to school, but her brothers did. Some people believe that Grace did go to school for a time at Spittal, as a boarder, but most of her education she received from her father. Mr Darling was himself a great reader. When asked about the loneliness of his life as a lighthouse keeper he would say,

'I'm never alone – I've always a book to read.'

The castle had a splendid library and Mr Darling was allowed to use it as often as he liked, and to take books back to the island. Grace later wrote in a letter to a friend, 'I have been brought up on the islands, learnt to read and write by my parents, and knit, spin and sew ... Our books are principally Divinity ... with a good many of the Religious Tract Society's publications ... and geography, history, voyages and travels, with maps, so that father can show us any part of the world, and give us a description of the people, manners and customs. So it is our own blame if we be ignorant of either what is done, or what ought to be done.'

Mr Darling was very musical and played the violin. On wet days he would march about the lighthouse whistling and fiddling while the younger children followed him in a skipping tail. He kept his own music book where he wrote out his favourite tunes – often ballads with names 'Stir Your Feet, Johnny', 'Whistle and I'll Come to You My Lad', 'Warm Broth' and 'Smash The Windows'.

There was, however, one yawning gap in the life of Grace and her brothers and sisters. She mentions it herself, in one of her letters later:

'Romances, novels and plays are books my father will not allow a place for in our house, for he says they are throwing away time.'

And so Grace heard the stories that people told of the old days, but never read fairy-tales or stories in books. At least, hardly ever...

Grace sat hunched in shawls, her face stinging with icy spray. Behind her she heard the creak of rowlocks as William and her father rowed steadily for shore. It was December and the sun was a red disc in a milky sky. Grace stared at the looming bulk of Bamburgh Castle ahead.

Is it true...? she wondered. Was it true about the Laidley Worm? If so, we're coming now just as Childe Wynde came to slay the dragon. Except that his boat had a keel of rowan-wood, to drive off the forces of evil...

She saw in her mind's eye the terrible worm with eyes the size and colour of lemons. She saw its leathery length coiled round the Spindlestone rock and –

'Grace! Grace! Wake up!' She heard her brother's voice and saw that they were there.

The three of them walked up the deserted beach right

under the shadow of the castle. As they entered the outer courtyard their footsteps rang in the frosty air and their mouths made little smokes.

Like the dragon's! thought Grace, and shivered.

William and her father went off to find Mr Smeddle. Robert was still at his lessons — they had come to fetch him home from school.

Grace, left to her own devices, wound through the maze of cold stone passages to the library. It was empty and hushed. Grace stared up at the rows of books.

As if in a spell, she thought. Waiting for someone to open them and bring them back to life!

She was moving towards the shelves when her eye fell on a book lying open on a table. On one page was a picture showing a maiden chained to a rock in the sea.

'Andromeda,' Grace read aloud. And then she sat down and began to read. She lost all count of time and was in another, enchanted world when she was brought to by the clanging of a bell. School was over.

'Oh no!' Grace could not bear it. If she got up now and left the book lying where she had found it, she might never see it again. And she would never know the end of the story. She had to know. She hesitated.

It would only be borrowing, she told herself. I'd bring it back next time we came.

And that was not the only thing. Her father would never let her take that book of stories to the island.

'Filling your head with such nonsense!' he would say. 'There's plenty of work to be done in the real world, without that!'

Still Grace hesitated.

Father went smuggling when he was young, she thought. He's often told us the tales of how he went out with the others on moonlit nights. If he can be a smuggler, why can't I?

She took the book and pushed it down into the deep pocket of her pinafore. Outside she could hear screams and laughter and clattering feet as the other children ran out from school. She peered out, standing on tiptoe, her chin on the stone sill. Below she could see the small charity girls in their blue dresses already making patterns over the courtyard, forming rings, starting games. Their voices floated up to her.

'Eeny weeny winey wo
Where do all the sailors go?
To the east and to the west
And into the old crow's nest!'

Grace went slowly down the stone passages, her hand closed over the book deep in her pocket. She walked out into the bitter, darkened air. The skipping and darting girls did not know that a smuggler had come among them.

There came a sudden roar and clatter of hobnailed boots. A gang of boys from the other school came rushing from their hiding-places in the castle corners.

'You're the Laidley Worm and I'm Childe Wynde!' they yelled, and brandished rulers as swords.

The girls shrieked and ran into little huddles. Only Grace was left standing alone. The boys advanced. Robert had told her of this game – a game for a boy to catch a girl and kiss her, as Childe Wynde had kissed Margaret.

'Kiss or kill! Kiss or kill!' The boys were advancing now in long strides while the girls squealed and giggled.

'*Got* you!' A boy jumped suddenly out behind Grace. She screamed and ran, past the shadowy huddles of girls and the capering boys, and now the voices of both boys and girls were chanting in unison:

'Run, run and the Worm'll get you! Run, run and the Worm'll get you!'

It was against the rules of the game to run off. Grace, filled with guilt and terror, could almost feel the hot breath of the monster and hear the slither of its coils over the icy stone. The voices were a long way off now, and she had run blindly down into a small deserted courtyard, one she could not remember seeing before.

'Turn and face it!' said a voice inside her head. She had come to a dead-end, there was nowhere to run to. She could sense the presence of that slimy, coiled thing. Her skin prickled with terror. Slowly, teeth gritted, she turned.

'Not there!'

Not to be seen, at any rate. Slowly, tiptoe almost, Grace retraced her steps and looked from left to right for a sign of tell-tale silvery scale or lidless yellow eye. That journey seemed a hundred miles, and all the way that stolen book burned in her pocket. Grace Darling had her stories, but she had paid for them.

CHAPTER

4

THE LONGSTONE

When Grace was eight or nine years old she noticed that there was more than the usual number of visitors to the Brownsman. Bearded men wearing the uniforms of Trinity House spent hours with her father, poring over maps and plans.

Grace knew that these visits were linked with the number of wrecks there had been lately. The brig *George and Mary* had struck the east point of the Brownsman in a snowstorm in February 1823 and all hands were lost. That same night the brig *Fortitude* was lost with all hands. The *August* struck rocks near Holy Island and all the crew were lost. The following year there were other wrecks on the Knavestone, Blue Caps, Megstone and Crumstone.

The Brownsman light was not high enough and not far enough out to sea. A new lighthouse was now being planned on the Longstone. The Brownsman light was only forty-three-feet high, but the new tower was to be almost a hundred-feet high, and circular. A smooth, circular structure afforded the least resistance to wind force and wave pressure in any direction.

In March 1825, Grace went out with her father to visit the Longstone, and saw that it was indeed long and indeed of stone. There was not a blade of grass to be seen. The island rose sheer out of the sea, but no more than about eight feet, so that at high tide and in strong gales the whole island was underwater. The crags were putty-coloured or greyish-green, and the lower stones barnacled like the hull of a ship. The surface of the island was rocky, the stones patched with a mustard-yellow crust and shining curls of seaweed.

Grace looked about her and saw that there would be no garden here, no goats and sheep, no rabbits, even. Her father read her thoughts.

'You walk down the other end,' he told her. 'You'll see something there.'

And so Grace picked her way over the rocks while the sea-birds screamed above her and the wind tugged at her skirt and apron so that they seemed to be dancing. She tucked her head down and planted her feet firmly, half afraid she might be blown away. On either side was the wide shine of the sea.

Soon we'll be all at sea, she thought. Might as well be a bird myself!

And then, all of a sudden, she saw the 'something' her father had promised.

Seals, hundred upon hundred of them, smooth and shining, pale-bellied and slithering from rock to sea. Great whiskered bull seals and lazily basking cows, and best of all the pups with the boot-button eyes and waving flippers. Grace stood and gazed, she watched for nearly an hour, and by the end of that time the Longstone no longer seemed so bleak and lonely.

'And think, Grace,' her father told her as they rowed back to the Brownsman, 'the very top room shall be yours! Right

up in the air with the birds you'll be. That'll suit you.'

Grace was filled with excitement. She was to have a room, a perfectly round room up in the sky with a bird's-eye view of the world. After that she often went out to the Longstone while the lighthouse was being built.

It was an enormous task. All the building materials had to be brought by boat. The billyboys or sloops came laden with stones from Yorkshire. The workmen had to stay on the island, and stone barracks were put up for them. Mr Nelson, the architect, and Thomas Wade, the foreman, stayed with the Darlings on the Brownsman.

The island of Longstone, never inhabited by humans since time began, was suddenly thronged. The haunt of wild birds was invaded by man. The ringing of hammers, the clash of iron and steel on stone, drove the birds off the islands nearby, terrified. It was nesting time. All through April, May and June the birds scattered to the outlying islands, the Pinnacles, the Inner Farne and Staple, to nest and rear their young. Grace watched forlornly over the grey-green summer waves and wondered if they would ever return. A world without birds was unthinkable.

Grace would stand and stare up at the huge stone structure rising higher each day till she was dizzy. She was waiting for the moment when at last that magical window that was to be hers appeared. When it did, she would gaze up at it until her neck cricked.

Then came the news that the Duke of Northumberland himself was to visit and inspect the lighthouse. The Duke was Admiral of that part of the coast, and had a very keen interest in lifesaving. His father had ordered the second lifeboat ever made and presented it to Shields with the money for its upkeep. There was now a lifeboat in Shields and one in Bamburgh itself.

The visit was made in September. The tower was nearly complete but the lantern had yet to be installed. All the Darling children were rowed over to the Longstone to meet the Duke. Grace, a new white pinafore over her best dress, wondered whether he would wear a crown and a velvet mantle. He was very tall and splendidly dressed and seemed very interested in the Darlings and the strange life they led. He asked questions about the garden on the Brownsman and about the birds. All these questions, Grace noticed, were to her brothers or to Mr Darling.

I know more about birds, she thought, and it was true. But she had to be content with a smile and a pat on the head.

When the Darlings moved out to the Longstone in Feb-

ruary 1826, they were taking a long stride out into the North
Sea. Their lives were lonelier than ever. There were no sheep
and goats, and though birds flew and screamed about the
island they could not breed there because of the high seas
continually covering the whole rock. Those seas came rushing
up the stone steps to the lighthouse itself, flooding the little
courtyard and threatening to come right into the kitchen. Life
was perilous and risky, it was like living in a sandcastle.

Mr Darling had been allowed to keep his garden on the
Brownsman but there were days, and even weeks on end,
when he could not visit it. Their lives were more than ever
governed by tides and weather.

The family shrunk as one by one the older children left for
life on shore. William left first, to work as a carpenter, then
Robert went to learn the trade of mason at Belford. Thomasin
and Mary Ann, who was now married, both lived in
Bamburgh. Betsy married and went to North Sunderland.
Grace kept in touch with them all by letter, but missed their
company, especially during the winter evenings. Then she
would sit in the kitchen with her mother and sew. Her
brothers sent boxes full of clothes home for mending, and
letters asking for new shirts and stockings. In the few hours
when he was not busy with his lantern, Mr Darling made
wooden inkstands and boxes to give as presents to his friends.

Grace would sit hour after hour in her round room at the
top of the tower. Below her the surf boiled and its roar was
ever-present as the air she breathed. And no one knows what
thoughts she had as she sat there, what dreams she may have
dreamt.

Mr Darling was kept busier than ever since the move.
There were the daily duties of the lantern, a regular routine
of tending his lamp. He would polish the reflectors, trim the
wicks and renew the oil. A pole had been installed to mark

the rise and fall of the tides, and he had to measure and note them for every hour of daylight. He also made notes of the times when the many treacherous, sunken rocks were covered.

Everything had to be kept shipshape at all times. The lighthouse regulations stated that everything must be kept in perfect order and repair, and the keepers themselves should be 'cleanly in their persons and linen, and orderly in their families'. At any time there could be a visit by a board member from Trinity House.

Water for drinking now had to be brought much further from the mainland and hoarded carefully. Rainwater was collected and stored in underground tanks, with a pump to bring it up to the scullery. But in dry spells supplies would run low. Grace writes in a letter to Thomasin:

'I have sent your caps that were made at Sunderland. You will be surprised when you see that I have sent them unwashed, but we are so badly off for water, we have five weeks' clothes dirty and not a drop of water to wash them with and only about two ankins in the well for dog or cat. I wish you could wish us to a good wet day.'

The lighthouse itself was at the eastern point of the island, with a lean-to boathouse and rocky steps leading down to the inlet where the coble was kept in good weather. All the rooms were circular. The kitchen, which was also the living-room, was at the base of the tower, and from it a spiral staircase wound up to the other rooms. There were three bedrooms, each becoming progressively smaller as the tower tapered, and Grace's, the topmost, was only ten feet in diameter.

There is a painting by Henry Parlee Parker, who often stayed with the family, that shows the kitchen in great detail. There is Mrs Darling's spinning-wheel and Mr Darling's guns, a grandfather clock, a sofa and armchairs. On a nail hangs

Mr Darling's watch, which he always took off when he went out in rough weather. Above the fireplace is a kettle hanging from a hook, and a shelf with salt-box, tea-caddy, flat-iron and oil lamp. The family's hats and straw bonnets hang from a rail. Strangely, the room is also crammed with stuffed birds. They perch everywhere, as if to show that as far as the Darlings were concerned, they were family.

Grace and her father both continued to study birds, and now that her brothers and sisters were away Grace often took an oar in the coble when they went on trips to the other islands. Sometimes they took naturalists, like Henry Hewitson.

Mr Darling was evidently not satisfied to live on an island without birds, even though they soared and screamed about him night and day, and nested close by on the Harcars and the Knavestone. He decided to do something about it. Fifteen years after he moved to the Longstone he was visited by William Howitt, who found to his amazement that the rock now had birds of its own. He described how this had come about:

'William Darling has laid sand for them along the ledge of rocks opposite to the lighthouse, and does not allow them to be plundered and so they haunt there in flocks of hundreds and make a continual noise, which I have no doubt in that solitude and in the absence of other living creatures is pleasant enough to him. He says none came there till he thus cared for them, and there are now hundreds which arrive in spring like other swallows, and stay the summer. Thus even wild creatures of the sea and air acknowledge kindness.'

Christmas 1834 there was the usual family gathering on the Longstone. William, now twenty-eight, was back, and his brothers Robert, twenty, and George Alexander, fifteen. Grace and her mother spent days baking and preparing the feast. It would be, they told each other, like the old times.

The brothers seemed to blow in from the mainland like a wind from the great outside world. Each had stories to tell, and Grace listened, half admiring, half wistful. She knew that she, as a girl, could never enter their world of adventure and excitement. It was for men to go out and fish and save lives on the sea, for women to stay at home and look after the men.

That Christmas, however, Grace herself was to play her first small part in saving the life of a man, that of James Logan. She was up in the lantern at eight o'clock on the morning of 28 December when she saw the figure of a man on the Knavestone rock. Down the steeply winding stairs she sped, her heart thudding, to tell her father. Mr Darling himself records the rescue briefly in his journal: '1834 Dec 27. Wind S. by E. fresh gale. 11 p.m. The sloop *Autumn* of and to Peterhead, with coals from Sunderland, struck east point of Knavestone and immediately sank. Crew of three men; two lost, one saved by the lightkeeper, and three sons, viz. William, Robert and George, after a struggle of three hours. Having lost two oars on the rock, had a very narrow escape.

PS The man saved, James Logan, stood near ten hours, part on the rock, part on the masthead, the mate lying dead beside him on the rock the last three hours, having perished from cold.'

That morning Grace saw her father and brothers go out with a stronger than usual sense of life and death, as if she knew how narrow an escape they would have. The men, still warm and sleepy from their beds, pulled on their things, their shadows lurching wildly about them.

'Oh dear, oh deary me!' Grace heard her mother mutter,
as she always did at such times. 'Lord save us, Lord save us!'

She embraced her husband, then each of her sons in turn.

'I'll have a good fire for when you're back, and plenty of
hot broth!'

She always said the same thing. It was a kind of charm,
Grace supposed. It was a way of blotting out the dark
and dangerous journey ahead and seeing her family back
safe again in her kitchen, hunched over bowls of steaming
broth.

As they opened the outer door the gale blew in. Grace
tasted the salt on her lips. The waves crashed at her very
feet. The coble had been put in the boathouse because of the
coming storm, and the men hurried to launch it. It was still
so dark that it was as if the dawn had never broken. Grace
watched them work, haloed in spray, and shivered.

But there's a man out there, she thought. A man, all alone,
clinging to the rock. If they don't go, he dies.

The thought that she hardly dared frame, the dread she
had felt all her life, was, They may not come back. I may
never see them again.

Now the coble was launched, already rocking dangerously.

'Farewell!' called Grace, but the words were blown back at
her and she swallowed them with the icy spray. She waved,
and saw an answering wave of the arm from one of the
shapes taking the oars. She did not know which.

Grace went back in and pushed the door shut against the
rude force of the gale and at once the world was muffled.
Mrs Darling was already busying herself, getting ready for
the return. She did the necessary things, like preparing food,
heating water, airing blankets. But she did unnecessary things
too, because she had to fill the long hours of waiting before
she saw her husband and sons safe again.

'What a thing, at Christmas!' Grace heard her say, as if the weather's manners left much to be desired.

'I'll go up and watch,' Grace said.

She began the steep, spiralling climb, her shadow curving on the walls. As she went it seemed that those very walls were shaking under the onslaught of the wind and waves.

What a thing, at Christmas! Mrs Darling's words ran in her head as she climbed, and then came a new thought, What if it hadn't happened at Christmas?

What if she, Grace Darling, had looked out and seen that lonely figure on the Knavestone, and all her brothers had been ashore?

She had reached the lantern now and the full force of the gale roared about her, rattling the glass, spattering it with spindrift. There was a thud as a bird, blown sideways, flew straight into the glass.

Grace shivered again and answered her own question.

'Then I should have had to go out with father.'

There, alone in the windswept tower, Grace Darling looked her worst fear in the face. It was as if all her life fear had been snapping at her heels, and now, for the first time, she turned and faced it. All the little fears – of the breathing trees in the Grove, the gallowing children on the dark sands, the loathsome Laidley Worm – had only been games, to distract her from the real terror, the nightmare.

'I'm only a girl,' she had told herself when her father and brothers went out to risk their lives. Her part was to help her mother prepare for their return. Her part was to nurse the shipwrecked sailors, to rinse and dry their sea-caked clothes, bind their wounds, feed them. She had even pretended to herself that she envied her brothers the chance to launch into boiling seas among perilous rocks.

Now she confronted the possibility of death square on.

She lifted the telescope to her eye. It was still there, that lonely figure on the Knavestone. She pictured the terrified man, his ship already sunk and his comrades drowned before his eyes. How he must be straining into the whipped-up spray for signs of rescue, how drenched and shivering he must be, his numb fingers clutching at the icy rock.

If Grace had seen that figure when all her brothers were ashore, then she would have no choice.

'I would have to go,' she told herself.

And from then onwards, life was simply a matter of waiting for that hour to come.

Years later, the youngest of the three brothers to go out that day, George Alexander, gave his account of what had happened:

When the *Autumn* struck on the night of the 27th December the Knavestone, which the sea covers at half or from that to three-quarters full tide, was still nearly underwater, although the tide fell. The vessel listed toward the rock, sank, and the Master with her. The mate, and the man Logan, first ascended to the topmast, which stood out above the water, and from thence they eventually scrambled on to the rock; but the mate died under exposure and was washed into a crevice by the returning tide. Logan remained alone, the tide rising.

About 8 o'clock on the morning of the 28th, Grace Darling, ere long to become the heroine of the Farne Islands, and then in her twentieth year, discerned him from the lantern of the Longstone. Her father had gone to rest for an hour or two, leaving Grace to put out the lights. She immediately roused him, and he and his said three sons got to the Knavestone.

Even in fine weather there are strong currents and a tossing sea above it, and with a high-flowing tide and a strong gale blowing, the risk run is apparent enough. There was no time to be lost. To attempt landing was out of the question. The Darlings tried to float a spar, with a rope attached, to Logan; but his condition had become frantic, and this was useless. Not much wonder, for when the boat was taken as near to him as it could be (dangerously near the rock) he stood up to his armpits in the tide. He gave such a leap as I shall never forget, and lay in the boat exhausted and silent. It was then that the two oars broke in the attempt to get away. Robert and George, the only two who could swim, had to quit the boat and help her off the rock. It was, even for them, imminent risk in such a sea, but they did it. It was a miracle that the boat was not destroyed, when all five must have perished.

Under a close-reefed sail, and taking a roundabout course, as they were by the gale compelled to do, at length they regained the Longstone lighthouse. It was not until Logan had been seven or eight hours in bed that he spoke for the first time about his rescue, and it was then only that particulars of the Mate's and Master's fate became known. The bodies were never recovered. Logan stated that the Master having his large boots on, they filled with water and prevented his escape to the topmast along with the other two.

Logan lay silent for many days in bed with a wide stare of terror as he relived his ordeal. It was weeks before he was fit to leave the Longstone. Then Mr Darling took him ashore to Bamburgh Castle. There Mr Smeddle gave orders for him to be fitted with new clothes and shoes. Mr Darling took him along the Belford road to catch the coach. Then Logan went on his way, and the Darlings never heard from him again.

CHAPTER
5

THE SHIPWRECK

On 5 September 1838 the steamship *Forfarshire* set sail from Hull to Dundee. It was carrying a heavy cargo and around sixty-three people, some forty of these being passengers. The *Forfarshire* was the queen of coastal steamers and lavishly fitted. As they wandered through the ship with its luxurious fittings, marble mantelpieces, gilt-edged mirrors, the passengers felt as much at home as in their own drawing-rooms — hardly at sea at all. They could no more imagine coming to harm here than by their own firesides.

One of the passengers was Mrs Dawson with her two children, a boy of eight and a girl of eleven. They were travelling steerage. The children raced all over the ship, mad with excitement, exploring the rich saloons and cabins.

'It's a floating palace!' they cried.

Who would have dreamt that a ship would have carpets, curtains, crystal glasses and silver cutlery laid on stiff white linen?

A lady sat in a plush chair in the Ladies' Salon, placidly dealing cards for patience. She looked up, watched the children gingerly touch a pyramid of fruit in a glass bowl to see if it was real, and smiled.

'Well,' she said. 'Is this not a fine ship?'

'Oh it is, it is! How fast shall we go?'

'And how would you like to visit the bridge, and stand at the side of the captain?'

Their eyes stretched. They would never have dared dream of such a thing.

'I am Mrs Humble,' she told them, 'and the captain is my husband. Ask your mother if you may go to the bridge, and I will arrange it.'

'Oh, thank you, thank you!'

Off they raced through that new, miniature world, to tell their mother.

'Say we can go!' they pleaded. 'Think – right on the bridge, next to the captain!'

And so the Dawson children went to stand on the bridge of the *Forfarshire* with Captain John Humble, and thought it the greatest moment of their lives.

'Stormy weather ahead,' the captain told them. 'Are you good sailors, I wonder?'

They shook their heads, not knowing. They had never been to sea before.

'We shan't — we shan't be wrecked, shall we?'

Captain John Humble laughed.

'On the *Forfarshire*? Never! We're steam, remember! Nothing can happen to the *Forfarshire*!'

And so he believed, his crew and passengers believed, and so certainly did the Dawson children.

Meanwhile Mr Darling, on the Longstone, grew anxious. It was the time of the equinoctial tides, and all through that Thursday the gale had strengthened.

'We shan't get to the Brownsman today,' he told Grace.

The potatoes must go undug, the goat unmilked. The journey was too risky. Brooks, now eighteen, had gone earlier over to Seahouses, and would not be able to get back. A thick grey mist came swirling in, and far away they heard the regular, melancholy boom of the great gun at Bamburgh Castle.

Grace went up to bed as usual in her round white room eighty feet above the boiling waves. It was secure and familiar as ever, cocooned from the wind and the weather. She looked about her at the collections of sea shells and birds' eggs in the flickering light of the candle. She twisted her ringlets into curling rags, put on her neat white nightdress and cap, and hung her gown of thin gingham, striped green and white, from a peg.

Last of all she peered from her window. She saw the pale yellow beam of the oil lamps slicing through the mist to the dark, jagged teeth of the Harcars.

Then Grace climbed into bed and lay for a while picturing sailors out there, battling with the mountainous seas. Above her head her father would keep the long night watches. Right from childhood she had been comforted by that steady light. Soon she was asleep.

Captain John Humble was himself keeping the night watch on the bridge of his ship. The weather, as he had warned the Dawson children, was wild, and steadily becoming worse. But the *Forfarshire* was not dependent on the weather as the old sail ships had been. She had steam.

It was about four o'clock on the Thursday morning that he received a report that the starboard boiler was leaking. Captain Humble hesitated. Should he put in to nearby Shields, or even return to Hull? But he had important first-class passengers aboard, and the reputation of the ship was at stake.

'The *Forfarshire* is queen!' he told himself. And then gave the order:

'Full steam ahead!'

As daylight came, thin and grey, the gales showed no sign of easing. Below, the pumps were working full out. The passengers too stayed below, and in the plush, carpeted saloons had only an inkling of the violence of the storm that was raging – except, of course, those who were seasick. The Dawson children were now pale and quiet. They lay and whimpered on their bunks while their mother soothed them.

'We shall soon be there,' she promised.

All day long they lay there, tossed by the violent squalls. In the end, worn out, they fell asleep, all three of them. They did not notice the ominous silence when at last, at one o'clock on the Friday morning, the engine gave a final throb and cut out. The *Forfarshire* had lost her steam.

*

Just after midnight Grace was awoken by a knocking at her door. Dazed, she saw her father, wearing his pilot coat and sealskin cap tied over his ears.

'I shall need you,' he told her. 'The wind's in the north now. There's no time to lose.'

He hurried down to set about clearing the courtyard and making everything fast. By four o'clock, he knew, the Longstone would be swamped by the highest tide they had ever known.

Grace quickly got up and dressed. She left her hair in its rags and snatched up a shawl. In the kitchen she took her bonnet from the rail and tied it tightly. She opened the door and was met by the full force of the gale and driving rain. It took her breath away. She made out the dim shape of her father, lashing the coble to its iron stanchions. He turned and saw her.

'Get those things in!' he roared.

Grace staggered here and there in the courtyard, her petticoats ballooning, the water already at her feet. She picked up the clothes-line and baskets and carried them back up the steps and into the kitchen. She and her father worked against time for nearly four hours. They hardly spoke, deafened as they were by the roar of wind and sea. The oars had to be made secure, the stepladders taken in and the garden tools. Then they carried up into the kitchen the rabbits in their hutches, the fishing tackle and baskets of apples. All the time they were buffeted by the wind and drenched with rain and spray. From time to time Grace raised her head and looked fearfully at the towering waves.

Just after four o'clock they had finished. Drenched and tired, they wordlessly pulled off their boots and outer clothes. Mrs Darling was up in the lantern, taking the last watch. At around six it would be dawn, and the lights could be put out.

Mr Darling went up to his bedroom and went straight to sleep.

Grace put her own shawl and her father's things before the fire and lingered for a few minutes, grateful for its blaze. Then she, too, went up to her room. Even more she loved its calmness and whiteness, a shelter from the storm. Her eyes went to the small round window, where she could see the silver splinters of rain in the light from the lantern. On impulse she went over and looked out.

She gasped. There, huge and impossible, was a ship. It seemed so close that she felt she could stretch out her hand and touch it. But it was on the Harcar reef, three hundred yards away. It was a giant wreck, ghost-like in the great blowing clouds of spindrift.

Grace ran down and roused her father. Still dazed from sleep, he rushed up to the lantern where his wife was dozing. He, too, could scarcely believe his own eyes. He groaned, and snatched up the telescope and began to scan the wreck for signs of life.

The *Forfarshire*, her power lost, was lashed by the wind and tide driving it landward. Captain Humble gave orders for the fore and aft sails to be raised. But the force of the gale was so tremendous that the helmsmen could not steer. The ship was drifting helplessly south.

Below the passengers slept or lay huddled on their bunks, frightened by the violent motion of the ship. The Dawson children woke and whimpered, their adventure turned to nightmare.

Captain Humble knew that they had passed the Berwick light, and decided that his best course was to steer for the Fairway, where they would be in more sheltered water till

the storm passed. He strained through the sheeting rain and mist for the revolving light of the Inner Farne. At last, around four o'clock, he caught a gleam, a faint twinkle.

'Anchors ready!' he roared, and the order passed round the ship. 'Anchors ready! Anchors ready!'

And then the captain stared aghast — straight ahead he saw the walls of white spray and the jagged cliffs of the Harcars.

'My God, we are all lost!'

He had mistaken the Longstone light for the Inner Farne.

He called down the companion, but only those nearest heard him. Crewmen ran to lower the starboard quarter boat and several of them, including the mate, jumped down into it and were immediately swept, without oars, into the open sea.

As they did so the ship was lifted by a giant roller and

crashed down on to the rock. There was a tremendous splintering. The cabin passengers, terrified, ran up on deck, and as they did so the ship was lifted and again smashed on to the rock. The *Forfarshire* was broken amidships. The stern part, together with Captain Humble and his wife and all the cabin passengers, was swept into the sea. All that rich plush, those marble mantels and gilded fittings were pulled into the sea like so many children's toys, lost for ever.

The fore part of the ship was left tilting dangerously on the rock. There were only twelve people now alive of the original sixty-three, five of whom were crew. There was a clergyman, the Reverend Mr Robb, James Kelly the weaver, Thomas Buchanan the baker, Daniel Donovan, who had been travelling free, and Mrs Dawson and her two children. They were left, drenched and terrified in the pitch-dark, clinging on for dear life while wave after wave threatened to wash them overboard.

The sailors struggled about the deck securing the survivors, lashing them firmly to masts and spars. One, the clergyman, refused to come up on deck, and as the tide rose was drowned in the forecabin. The rest, now unable to move and mercilessly dashed by the sea and driving rain, could only wait and pray until the dawn.

When day broke they saw the rock on which they had foundered and the danger of their position on the shattered and ominously creaking wreck. One by one the sailors helped the passengers down on to the rock itself, where at least they were safe from being swept away. They handed the shuddering Dawson children down into the arms of their mother. They moved the body of The Reverend Mr Robb. In the bleak dawn light those eleven huddled, lost and deafened in a world of icy spray. Each one silently wondered which would come first – rescue or death.

THE DEED

As that same dawn broke the phantom hulk of the *Forfarshire* was seen to be only too real. Grace saw its broken masts and spars thrusting into the mist and spindrift. Then, after nearly a full two hours of straining into the spray and darkness, she and her father saw the first signs of life.

Grace, seeing those forlorn figures on the black rock, knew that her hour had come.

She wrote afterwards:

'I had little thought of anything but to exert myself to the utmost, my spirit was worked by the sight of such a dreadful affair that I can imagine I can still see the sea flying over the vessel.'

Grace and her father both knew that they must go. They must unlash the coble, and in that small boat attempt the dangerous crossing.

Grace ran to her room and pulled off all her petticoats. She wound a plaid shawl tightly round her neck then crossed and tied it behind her waist, to leave her arms free. Again she tied her bonnet over her head, curling rags and all. Then, with one last look at her calm white room, she ran down the winding stairs.

Mrs Darling had prepared breakfast and coffee but Grace and her father would not wait. Every second was precious. Mrs Darling, who had seen her husband go out in many a storm, was seized with terror. It seemed impossible that he could make that journey safely in the small coble. She wept and implored him not to go.

In the end she had to go out with them, in her frilled mob-cap and thin shawl, to steady the coble as they climbed in. Her last words were, 'Oh, Grace, if your father is lost, I'll blame a' you for this morning's work!'

Then, for Grace, there was nothing but the roar and thunder of the waves. The great grey walls now towered above and then, next moment, she seemed poised above a chasm. She sat amidships with her father, each pulling an oar. They rode on a great sea full twenty fathoms deep.

The Harcars lay only three hundred yards away, tantalizingly close. But to reach them the Darlings had to row a mile, in the lee of the Blue Caps. All that long journey they were blinded by driving rain, yet knew they were steering through treacherous rocks that might at any moment overturn them. Although it was past dawn it was still so dark it might have been the end of the world.

The coble needed three men to row her in rough seas, and these were seas beyond imagination. Grace, with her slender wrists, had to pull on the heavy oar to match her father. Perhaps she did not have time to feel terror, to dread her own death by drowning.

When at last they drew near to the reef the wreck loomed above them, a huge shape in the mist. Now they could see the people clinging for dear life on to the rock, while great clouds of spray broke over them.

Above the roar of wind and surf they heard a man's cry:
'For the Lord's sake, there's a lassie coming!'

Mr Darling saw at once that there were too many survivors
to take off at once. A second trip, equally hazardous, would
have to be made. The frantic people were now shouting and
screaming, scrambling to reach the coble first. All but the still
figure of a man lying on the gleaming rock, and two small
shapes lying limply in their mother's arms. The Dawson
children were dead.

Mr Darling acted swiftly. He knew that he could not take
all the howling and pleading survivors at once. Somehow he
must reason with them. With the next high wave he himself
leapt out on to the rock. Grace was left alone in the coble.

As an old man, Mr Darling said that those had been the
worst moments of his life, when he had had to leave his
daughter all alone in the boat, frail as a matchstick in those
violent waves.

Grace's own heart stopped as she saw her father leap. She
hardly believed her eyes. Now the lives of all of them
depended on her. She clutched at her father's oar before it
could be washed away. She knew what she must do to keep
the coble off the rocks, or from being swept away altogether.

Those minutes when Grace, a tiny figure in her drenched
clothes and bonnet, held the coble alone, were the longest of
her life. She gasped as wave after wave struck the rocks,
pitching the boat and blinding her with icy spray. All the
time she held tightly on to both oars and desperately rowed
backwards and forwards as quickly as possible, to keep the
coble steady.

Her father swiftly selected the first boatload – the woman,
a sick man and three of the crew. Grace pulled in the boat as
close as she dared. Mrs Dawson, moaning and pleading to
be left with her children, was lifted in, then the injured man.

The others, waist-high in water, struggled aboard. Grace gave her oar to one of the sailors, and the dangerous trip back to the lighthouse began. Mr Darling later described it:

'Grace sat in the midships, the woman sat upon flooring forward with her head lying against the side, as she was not fit to sit on the seats, and one of the men was lying aft in the same manner, with a blanket round each. Four oars used in pulling back, no rudder was shipped.'

When at last they reached the Longstone, Grace and the woman and injured man were landed, but her father and two of the sailors turned straight back to the wreck to bring off the others. Grace's work was not yet done. Exhausted as she was, she helped her mother all through that dark day. Mrs Dawson was helped up the tower and into Grace's own room, where she stayed for three days, while Grace herself slept on the table.

The shipwrecked men were all cut and bruised and shocked. They were given dry clothing and hot broth. The most seriously injured were put in the big room lined with bunks, used by Grace's brothers when they were home. The rest were bedded down on the floor by the kitchen fire. All were exhausted yet their eyes still stared wide with terror.

The storm, now muffled by the thick walls of the light-house, still raged. Mr Darling knew that there was no hope of taking the survivors ashore, possibly for days. All nine of them would have to be fed and cared for on the Longstone.

As Grace moved among the stricken sailors, bathing their wounds and listening to their delirious ravings, her parents held a worried consultation. Provisions were already low. A trip even to the Brownsman for supplies was out of the question. How would they hold out?

It was at this moment that the kitchen door burst open. They whirled round, half expecting to be engulfed by waves. There, framed in the doorway, was their son Brooks!

Beside him was his friend, William Swan, the Trinity boatman, and behind him five other members of the North Sunderland lifeboat crew. They were drenched and weary, and stared incredulously at the crowded scene in the kitchen. The Darlings, equally thunderstruck, stared back.

The North Sunderland men had gone out!

When William Darling had set out with Grace to the wrecked *Forfarshire* he had believed it impossible that either the Bamburgh or the North Sunderland lifeboat should be launched. But during the two hours up in the lantern when Mr Darling was scanning the wreck for signs of life, the vessel had been sighted from the look-out turret at Bamburgh Castle.

Mr Smeddle, agent of the Crewe Trustees, had ordered the flag to be hoisted half-mast high and a thirty-two pounder fired, as a signal that the wreck had been sighted. Then, at dawn, he set off on horseback through the driving rain to alert the men of the North Sunderland lifeboat.

He reached Seahouses at seven. There he found the fishermen already at the harbour. During the night the waves had washed right over the breakwater and the cottages at the quayside. The men were now working fast to save the herring barrels on the quay, many of which had already been swept away. Mr Smeddle gasped out his news, and summoned the lifeboatmen to launch the lifeboat.

They did not hesitate. They knew that their craft was light and shallow, that it could easily be overturned in such a gale. But William Brooks Darling was there, and he knew the rocks and currents of the Outer Farnes, had known them in all weathers. He was first to jump into a coble. With him went six others, three of them brothers — William, James and Michael Robson. Their mother, already a widow, wept as she saw them go. The boat was launched at almost exactly the same time as Grace and her father were setting off from the Longstone.

The journey they made to the Harcars was longer and even more perilous than that made by Grace and her father. It took a full two and a half hours, all the time shipping heavy seas. When they reached the wreck they found not a living soul. They had arrived too late.

They moved the bodies of the minister and the two Dawson children higher up the rock, well beyond reach of the waves. The storm was as fierce as ever, and they were by now exhausted. Instead of attempting the long haul back to Seahouses, they decided to make for the Longstone. There they would find safety and shelter, dry clothes, warmth and food.

And so they made for the lighthouse. The seas by the

steps where Grace and her father had launched their coble were now boiling so fiercely that if they had tried to land, their boat would have been smashed to pieces. So they made for Sunderland Hole, on the leeward side. They managed to land their boat and pull her up to safety, and lurched over the slippery rock of the island towards the lighthouse.

There they found the people they had set out to save and had thought lost. Dazed as they were, they could hardly believe their eyes. Still less could they believe their ears when they were told that Grace, a mere girl, had gone out with her father in those tremendous seas. Never in all their lives had they heard of such a thing.

They had found shelter of a kind, but there was no room for them in the lighthouse itself, filled as it was to overflowing. And so for two days they had to stay in the barracks that had been put up for the workmen twelve years before when the lighthouse was built. By now, buffeted by wind and tide, it was in ruins. The roof was half gone, they could not even light a fire. During those two days at each high tide the lifeboatmen were forced to leave the barracks and crowd into the lighthouse until the tide ebbed. There they were given their meagre rations of food while Mrs Darling anxiously watched her rapidly vanishing stores.

Grace and her mother worked ceaselessly, heating water, cooking, drying clothes and bedding, tending wounds. On the third day the storm abated. At evening the lifeboatmen decided to risk making for land, taking with them the bodies of the clergyman and the Dawson children.

Grace climbed wearily up the tower to watch them go. Softly she opened the door of her room. There, motionless on the bed, lay Mrs Dawson, moaning for her dead children. Grace looked about her at the round, white-walled room with its birds and shells, and felt as if she had been away for a thousand years. She moved towards the round window and stared out through the grey mist and spindrift at the ghostly hulk of the *Forfarshire*. Her mind was as numb as her limbs, but even so she was dimly aware that some enormous change had been wrought since last she had slept in this calm round room. Neither she, nor the world, would ever be the same again.

FAME

Grace could never have dreamed of the fame that was to follow. The news of her deed was slow to spread. It was not until the Sunday that the lifeboatmen of Sunderland brought the news to the mainland. Those on shore knew of the wreck but had no idea of how many lives had been saved or lost. There was no telephone or wireless, news usually went by coach or horseman, who would travel at the rate of about twelve miles an hour. Bamburgh is three hundred and thirty-five miles from London.

It was the local papers therefore which first carried the story. The reporters were rowed out to the Longstone, agog at this amazing tale of a slight girl who had lived all her life on a solitary rock and had shown such amazing courage.

When they reached the island they found Grace and her mother hard at work, clearing up after those three crowded days at the lighthouse. They embarked upon a huge wash of all the sheets, blankets, pillowcases and towels. The living-room was filled with the smell of soap and steam. Nearly all their supplies had gone – all the cured herrings, bacons, hams, peasemeal and barley. They were working to get things back to normal, little knowing that as far as Grace herself was concerned, life would never be normal again.

One of the earliest reports was from the *Sunderland Herald*:

... as we approached the lighthouse the heroine, Grace Darling herself, was descried high aloft, lighting the lamps, whose revolving illumination has warned many an anxious mariner of the rocks and shoals around. We were met at the door of the hospitable tower, and received a hearty welcome from old Mrs Darling and her dauntless daughter. But Grace is nothing masculine in her appearance although she has so stout a heart. In person she is about the middle size, of a comely countenance – rather fair for an islander – and with an expression of benevolence and softness most truly *feminine* in every point of view. When we spoke of her noble and heroic conduct she slightly blushed and appeared anxious to avoid the notice to which it exposed her; she smiled at our praise but said nothing in reply ...

It was a full fortnight after the wreck when *The Times* came out with the article that overnight made Grace a national heroine:

'It is impossible to speak in adequate terms of the unparalleled bravery and disinterestedness shown by Mr Darling and his truly heroic daughter, especially so with regard to the latter. Is there in the whole field of history, or of fiction even, one instance of female heroism to compare for one moment with this?'

From that moment Grace's place in history was certain. A fund was set up for her and contributions poured in. Her name was the toast of public dinners and mayoral banquets up and down the land. All kinds of vessels were named after her, and her name was carried on their prows to all parts of the world.

Requests for autographs flooded in. She wrote to a friend,

'According to your request you will receive a few signa-
tures, but you must not promise them too many, for I am
both 'deed swere and unco' ill o'. Perhaps you would scarcely
believe it, I have signed about a hundred and ten cards for
Mr Smeddle alone, and I don't know how many to others.'

In those days it was quite common for admirers to ask for a
lock of hair. Had Grace sent as many locks as were requested
she would very soon have been bald. Soon shops began to
sell locks that were supposed to be Grace's, and one of her
brothers, George Alexander, was being shaved in a barber's
in Newcastle when a man hawking a trayful of hair invited
him to buy a lock. When asked what he did he replied tersely,

'Kicked the man out o' the shop! It was no hair o' Gracie's!'

One newspaper reported,

This humane and heroic female received a letter a few days ago
from a lady at Alnwick, enclosing a five-pound note and requesting
in return a lock of her hair. Several ladies who have recently visited
the Farne Islands have solicited and obtained similar tokens of
remembrance; and there seems a probability, if the demand should
continue, that she will ere long have to seek an artificial, in exchange
for the natural, covering of her head – unless indeed by the use of
bears' grease or Macassar oil she should succeed in producing a
regular succession of crops. It appears somewhat absurd to endeav-
our thus to deprive Miss Darling of her ringlets, but it at the same
time shows that her humanity and heroism have made a deep
impression on those who are desirous of possessing them.

Grace began to receive gifts. She was sent a beautiful wooden
workbox, bibles and other books, gold and precious rings, a
Paisley shawl and half a dozen silver teaspoons. Mrs Darling
was even sent a cream jug inscribed 'To the Mother of Grace
Darling'. Grace was sent a special hat by a hatmaker in
Berwick. It was a bonnet of black beaver, and she sat for

portraits wearing it and so set a fashion. All that winter ladies wore the Grace Darling Hat.

Then there were the souvenir hunters. Boats were rowed out to search for fragments of the wreckage. Even rusted nails were mounted and treasured and handed down through families. Next came the manufacture of souvenirs and knick-knacks. There were Staffordshire mugs bearing her portrait in colour, a Staffordshire figure of Grace and her father, coloured pictures for children to cut out and paste on nursery screens.

Artists came out to the island, eager to paint Grace's portrait or to depict the rescue itself. Photography was then only in its infancy. These artists often had to stay on the Longstone for quite long periods, and at one time there were no fewer than seven of them staying at the lighthouse. Here Mr Darling drew the line. He wrote to one artist who requested a visit that they had posed to eleven artists in the last fortnight, and 'it would require for them to have nothing else to do!'

Poems and ballads were written in Grace's honour by William Wordsworth and Algernon Swinburne, as well as other less famous writers. Most of these are very bad, and they are usually inaccurate.

Honours were bestowed. Silver medals were presented to Grace and her father by the Royal National Institute for the Preservation of Life from Shipwreck. Later they were given the highest award ever granted by the National Royal Humane Society, their Gold Medal, accompanied by inscribed vellum scrolls. They were first summoned to Alnwick Castle to meet the Duke of Northumberland, and then, at Christmas, a surprise box arrived at the island. In it were gifts from the Duke, and a list of contents in his own handwriting on gilt-edged notepaper:

List of things sent in the box to Wm. Darling:

Medal from the Shipwreck Society at Newcastle.

A coat-jacket-trousers and cloth for D. of waterproof cloth.

Two votes of thanks on vellum (framed) from the Humane Society.

FOR MRS DARLING:

A silver teapot to be constantly used by her, and afterwards to belong to Grace H. Darling.

Camlet cloak waterproof.

4 lbs tea. (Turn over.)

FOR GRACE HORSLEY DARLING:

A silver-gilt watch with a gold seal and two keys.

A medal from Shipwreck Society at Newcastle.

Camlet cloak waterproof.

A prayer book with the daily lessons from the Old and New Testaments.

Volume with the best notes to accompany the Bible.

One of the vellum notes of the Humane Society.

NB The two medals, the watch seal and the keys are in the inside of Mrs Darling's teapot.

The prayer book sent by her guardian may be very convenient to those who are detained at the lighthouse on Sundays.

The notes on the Bible are the best that have been published.

To Grace Horsley Darling, Longstone Lighthouse.   N.

The outside world had never been very real to Grace. Now it crowded in on all sides. Besides the constant stream of letters and visitors to the island, there were pageants and plays performed about her in London and the provinces. Grace was even offered a large sum of money by the manager of the Adelphi Theatre, just to come to London and sit in a boat on the stage for a quarter of an hour.

All this must have seemed curiously unreal to Grace herself.

She had, on one single occasion, risen to extraordinary heights of courage. This was what the world thought of whenever her name was mentioned.

But the real Grace Darling had lived a life that was itself extraordinary, and that life the world could hardly imagine. For over twenty years she had lived on solitary rocks in the North Sea. The pattern of her days was woven with sea, wind and weather. The only crowds she ever knew were of the sea-birds she loved and studied. How could an outsider picture what it meant to wake each morning in a round white room eighty feet above the sea? In mist and rain, wind and sun, she was always surrounded by scenes of a strange wild beauty.

And so perhaps Grace Darling, feeling that the world praised her without really knowing her, began to feel unreal. Her inner self, as well as the Longstone Island, was invaded.

Whatever the reason, after only a few years of a life that was crowded when once it had been solitary, Grace fell ill. In the early spring of 1842 she caught a chill during a visit to the mainland. It is curious that a girl who had all her life been used to icy drenchings from the North Sea should catch a fatal chill in Harrowgate.

From that time Grace never recovered her health. As she grew worse she was taken from her natural home on the Longstone and brought to Bamburgh. In those days doctors believed that fresh air was bad for delicate patients. Grace was kept shut up in stuffy rooms by well-meaning relatives and friends. She was taken to her sister's on the dark side of the street by the Grove. In winter months no sun ever strikes the windows, which were kept tightly shut, for fear of draught.

Grace Darling, whose elements were the sea and sky, was placed in a box bed with sliding doors. It might have been a

coffin. As she lay there she must have consoled herself with daydreams of the old days on the Brownsman and Longstone. She must have had memories of shining silver shoals of herrings, of wild sunsets and the silent terns beating in procession out over the waves.

On 20 October 1842 Grace Darling died in her father's arms and a whole nation went into mourning.

EPILOGUE

Go to Bamburgh and you will find it very much as it was in Grace Darling's lifetime. St Aidan's Church, Job Horsley's cottage, the Grove, the castle and the Wynding are all there, a century and a half of wind and weather the worse for wear. Opposite the churchyard, with Grace's own effigy among the barnacled stones, is the Grace Darling Museum.

There you can see the coble in which she and her father rowed out to the *Forfarshire*. There are some of Grace's own belongings — shawls, samplers — even a piece of the green-and-white striped cotton dress she was wearing that fateful day. There is the wall clock from Grace's room in the Long-stone — cream, with painted roses, a brass face and hands and Roman numerals. You can see the Darlings' key baskets, telescopes, pewter flasks, wooden cradle with curved hood and rockers.

But if you really want to understand Grace Darling and how she lived, you must visit Seahouses, just down the coast. There you can find a boat to take you out to the islands. Once out at sea you will begin to look at the world through Grace's eyes. You will be surrounded by screaming sea-birds and the boatmen will point them out to you – the kittiwakes, cormorants, guillemots, razorbills. You will pass the Brownsman and the whitened rocks of the Pinnacles with their thousands of puffins. Colonies of seals will be basking and if the sea is calm the boat will go close up so that you can almost touch them.

Then you can land on the Longstone. The lighthouse has been modernized now, but the structure is exactly as it was in Grace Darling's day. You can actually stand on the steps from which the coble was launched. Then climb the winding stairs and you will be able to walk into Grace's own round room eighty feet above the sea, and look out of the very window through which she saw the wreck of the *Forfarshire*, ghostly in the spindrift.

Now you are at last seeing the world through the eyes of Grace Darling. Here she spent hours and days and years with only the implacable waves and the sea-birds as company. Think of the stoical rising in cold dawns to days filled with unrelenting duties. There was the bleak, windswept garden on the Brownsman to tend, fish to be caught and salted, cloth to be woven. Imagine the dark storms of winter, the North Sea coming right to the kitchen door, food and water running dangerously low.

Above all, there was the patient, ceaseless climbing of those stone steps up to the lantern that must be kept burning, year in year out. Imagine all this, and you might decide, as I myself have come to believe, that Grace Darling was not a heroine simply because of that one famous deed of courage on 7 September 1838. She lived as a heroine every day of her life.

RNLI GRACE DARLING APPEAL

To mark the 150th anniversary of Grace Darling's epic rescue, the Royal National Lifeboat Institution has launched the Grace Darling Appeal. The aim is to raise enough money to fund a new lifeboat for North Sunderland lifeboat station, to be called *Grace Darling*. Fund raising and project ideas are available for schools. For further information write to: Grace Darling Appeal, RNLI, West Quay Road, Poole, Dorset, BH15 1HZ.

STORM FORCE

Storm Force is the RNLI's exciting junior membership club for young people under sixteen years of age. Members receive a certificate, poster, badge, stickers and *Storm Force News* four times a year. Individual membership costs £3.00 a year and groups of ten or more can join for £1 each.

Find out more by writing to:

Storm Force HQ, RNLI, West Quay Road, Poole, Dorset, BH15 1HZ.

THE LANDFILL *David Leney*

Danny is angry when he discovers his safe, private world among the junk at the landfill has been invaded. But he has no idea that something as innocent as a story recorded on a cassette could have such a dramatic effect on his life.

ALL THE WAY TO WIT'S END *Sheila Greenwald*

Drucilla Brattles has had enough! She's fed up with being surrounded by antiques and heirlooms and she's fed up with wearing ancient dresses. She yearns for a new life: for soft carpets and a cosy home; for decent clothes and for a brace for her teeth, so she'll be able to close her mouth!

Then she hatches a plan, an incredible scheme which turns everyone's lives upside down!

GAMES . . . *Robin Klein*

A ramshackle, eerie and isolated house, set on the fringe of the Australian bush, seems an ideal venue for a weekend party to Kirsty and Genevieve – particularly when the owner, Kirsty's aunt, is known to be away. Poor Patricia Miggs, more of an afterthought than a friend, tries desperately to win their approval now that she has the honour of their company. However, the fears that she holds for her lack of social graces are as nothing compared to the sheer terror that engulfs all three once the party is abandoned and the games begin . . .

THE FINDING *Nina Bawden*

Alex doesn't know his birthday because he was found abandoned next to Cleopatra's Needle, so instead of a birthday he celebrates his Finding. After inheriting an unexpected fortune, Alex's life suddenly becomes very exciting indeed.

BOY and GOING SOLO *Roald Dahl*

The enthralling autobiography of this much loved author, from his earliest days to his experiences as a pilot in the Second World War.

THE APPRENTICES *Leon Garfield*

A collection of the much-acclaimed Apprentices stories. Each story features one London trade and is linked by recurring characters.

THE BONNY PIT LADDIE *Frederick Grice*

Set in the early 20th century, this story of a boy growing up in a mining village was one of the first children's books to show real working-class children in credible surroundings.

SARAH, PLAIN AND TALL *Patricia MacLachlan*

What would she be like, this new mother found through a newspaper advertisement? And above all, would she be able to sing?

COME BACK SOON *Judy Gardiner*

Val's family seem quite an odd bunch and their life is hectic but happy. But then Val's mother walks out on them and Val's carefree life is suddenly quite different. This is a moving but funny story.

AMY'S EYES *Richard Kennedy*

When a doll changes into a man it means that anything might happen . . . and in this magical story all kinds of strange and wonderful things do happen to Amy and her sailor doll, the Captain. Together they set off on a fantastic journey on a quest for treasure more valuable than mere gold.

ASTERCOTE *Penelope Lively*

Astercote village was destroyed by plague in the fourteenth century and Mair and her brother Peter find themselves caught up in a strange adventure when an ancient superstition is resurrected.

THE HOUNDS OF THE MÓRRÍGAN *Pat O'Shea*

When the Great Queen Mórrígan, evil creature from the world of Irish mythology, returns to destroy the world, Pidge and Brigit are the children chosen to thwart her. How they go about it makes an hilarious, moving story, full of original and unforgettable characters.

COME SING, JIMMY JO *Katherine Paterson*

An absorbing story about eleven-year-old Jimmy Jo's rise to stardom, and the problem of coping with fame.

JELLYBEAN *Tessa Duder*

A sensitive modern novel about Geraldine, alias 'Jellybean', who leads a rather solitary life as the only child of a single parent. She's tired of having to fit in with her mother's busy schedule, but a new friend and a performance of 'The Nutcracker Suite' change everything.

THE PRIESTS OF FERRIS *Maurice Gee*

Susan Ferris and her cousin Nick return to the world of O which they had saved from the evil Halfmen, only to find that O is now ruled by cruel and ruthless priests. Can they save the inhabitants of O from tyranny? An action-packed and gripping story by the author of prize-winning THE HALFMEN OF O.

THE SEA IS SINGING *Rosalind Kerven*

In her seaside Shetland home, Tess is torn between the plight of the whales and loyalty to her father and his job on the oil rig. A haunting and thought-provoking novel.

BACK HOME *Michelle Magorian*

A marvellously gripping story of an irrepressible girl's struggle to adjust to a new life. Twelve-year-old Rusty, who had been evacuated to the United States when she was seven, returns to the grey austerity of post-war Britain.

THE BEAST MASTER *André Norton*

Spine-chilling science fiction – treachery and revenge! Hosteen Storm is a man with a mission to find and punish Brad Quade, the man who killed his father long ago on Terra, the planet where life no longer exists.

FRYING AS USUAL *Joan Lingard*

Disaster strikes the Francettis when Mr Francetti breaks his leg. Their fish and chip shop never closes, but who is going to run it now that he's in hospital and their mother is in Italy? The answer is quite simple to Toni, Rosita and Paula, and with the help of Grandpa they decide to carry on frying as usual. But it's not that easy . . .

THE FREEDOM MACHINE *Joan Lingard*

Mungo dislikes Aunt Janet and to avoid staying with her he decides to hit the open road and look after himself, and with his bike he heads northwards bound for adventure and freedom. But he soon discovers that freedom isn't quite what he's expected, especially when his food supplies are stolen, and in the course of his journey he learns a few things about himself.

KING DEATH'S GARDEN *Ann Halam*

Maurice has discovered a way of visiting the past, and whatever its dangers it's too exciting for him to want to give up – yet. A subtle and intriguing ghost story for older readers.

STRAW FIRE *Angela Hassall*

Kevin and Sam meet Mark, an older boy who is sleeping rough up on the Heath behind their street. Kevin feels there is something weird about Mark, something he can't quite put his finger on. And he is soon to discover that there is something very frightening and dangerous about Mark too.

THE PRIME MINISTER'S BRAIN   *Gillian Cross*

The fiendish Demon Headmaster plans to gain control of No. 10 Downing Street and lure the Prime Minister into his evil clutches.

JASON BODGER AND THE PRIORY GHOST
Gene Kemp

A ghost story, both funny and exciting, about Jason, the bane of every teacher's life, who is pursued by the ghost of a little nun from the twelfth century!

HALFWAY ACROSS THE GALAXY AND TURN LEFT   *Robin Klein*

A humorous account of what happens to a family banished from their planet Zygron, when they have to spend a period of exile on Earth.

SUPERGRAN TO THE RESCUE   *Forrest Wilson*

The punchpacking, baddiebiffing escapades of the world's No. 1 senior citizen superhero – Super Gran! Now a devastating series on ITV!

TOM TIDDLER'S GROUND   *John Rowe Townsend*

Vic and Brain are given an old rowing boat which leads to the unravelling of a mystery and a happy reunion of two friends. An exciting adventure story.

JUNIPER *Gene Kemp*

Since her dad left Juniper and her mum have had nothing but problems and now things are just getting worse – there are even threats to put Juniper into care. Then she notices two suspicious men who seem to be following her. Who are they? Why are they interested in her? As Christmas draws nearer Juniper knows something is going to happen . . .

RACSO AND THE RATS OF NIMH
Jane Leslie Conly

When fieldmouse Timothy Frisby rescues young Racso, the city rat, from drowning, it's the beginning of a friendship. It's also the beginning of Racso's education – and an adventure. For the two are caught up in the brave and resourceful struggle of the Rats of NIMH to save Thorn Valley, their home, from destruction.

A TASTE OF BLACKBERRIES
Doris Buchanan Smith

The moving story about a young boy who has to come to terms with the tragic death of his best friend and the guilty feeling that he could somehow have saved him.